READY AND WAITING FOR YOU

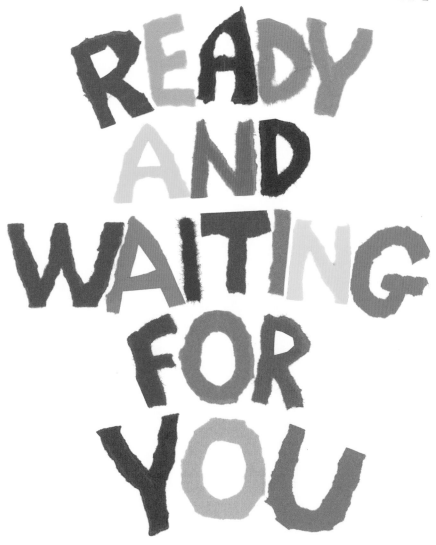

Written by
Judi Moreillon

Illustrated by
Catherine Stock

Eerdmans Books for Young Readers

Grand Rapids, Michigan • Cambridge, U.K.

For Gavin, Little Clive, and all of the children whose
lives are touched by caring educators around the world
who joyfully open the doors to learning.
— J. M.

Pour Sophie
— C. S.

Text © 2013 Judi Moreillon
Illustrations © 2013 Catherine Stock

Published in 2013 by Eerdmans Books for Young Readers,
an imprint of Wm. B. Eerdmans Publishing Co.
2140 Oak Industrial Dr. NE
Grand Rapids, Michigan 49505
P.O. Box 163, Cambridge CB3 9PU U.K.

www.eerdmans.com/youngreaders

Manufactured at Tien Wah Press
in Malaysia in February 2013, first printing

19 18 17 16 15 14 13   9 8 7 6 5 4 3 2 1

The open door design concept for this book was created by Judi Moreillon.
The illustrations were rendered in torn paper.
The display type was hand constructed by Catherine Stock.
The text type was set in Massif.

Library of Congress Cataloging-in-Publication Data

Moreillon, Judi.
Ready and waiting for you / by Judi Moreillon;
illustrated by Catherine Stock.
pages cm
Summary: "Warm and friendly characters welcome a new
student to the first day of school" — Provided by publisher.
ISBN 978-0-8028-5355-4
[1. First day of school — Fiction. 2. Schools — Fiction.]
I. Stock, Catherine, illustrator. II. Title.
PZ7.M78946Re 2013
[E] — dc23
2012049250

Your boisterous bus mates and the bus driver say,

"We're ready and waiting for you."

Come in. Come in.
Come in through this door.

Are you new?

The helpful crossing guards, babies in strollers,
and neighborhood dogs too —

everyone's waiting for you!

Your proud principal and
the school mascot say,

"We're ready and waiting for you."

Come in. Come in.
Come in through this door.

Are you new?

OFFICE

The school secretary,
the attendance clerk,
and the school nurse too —

everyone's waiting for you!

Come in. Come in.
Come in through this door.

Are you new?

Your savvy librarian and
your computer tech say,

"We're ready and waiting for you."

The gym teacher, the art teacher,
and the music teacher too —

everyone's waiting for you!

Come in. Come in.
Come in through this door.

Are you new?

Your cafeteria cooks and
your food workers say,

"We're ready and waiting for you."

The playground monitors,
the custodians,
and the parent volunteers too —

everyone's waiting for you!

Come in. Come in.
Come in through this door.

Are you new?

Your clever classmates and
your friendly teacher say,

"We're ready and waiting for you."

Come in. Come in.
Come in through this door . . .

We won't be a whole school till you do.

Everyone's waiting for you!

See You Soon!